Disney's Winnie the Pooh

A Bear-y Good Neighbor

D0598694

By Kathleen W. Zoehfeld
Illustrated by Robbin Cuddy

A Random House PICTUREBACK® Book

Copyright © 1997, 2001 by Disney Enterprises, Inc. Based on the Pooh stories by A. A. Milne (Copyright The Pooh Properties Trust).
All rights reserved under International and Pan-American Copyright Conventions. Published in the United States by Random House, Inc.,
New York, and simultaneously in Canada by Random House of Canada Limited, Toronto, in conjunction with Disney Enterprises, Inc.
Originally published in slightly different form by Disney Press in 1997 as *Pooh's Neighborhood*.
Library of Congress Catalog Card Number: 00-107381   ISBN: 0-7364-1108-9
www.randomhouse.com/kids/disney   www.disneybooks.com
Printed in the United States of America   January 2001   10 9 8 7 6 5 4 3 2 1
PICTUREBACK, RANDOM HOUSE and colophon, and PLEASE READ TO ME and colophon are registered trademarks of Random House, Inc.

"I say, it's a splendid day in the neighborhood!" said Owl.

"Which neighbor wood are we talking about?" asked Pooh.

"Neighbor*hood*," said Owl. "*Our* neighborhood—the place where we live and where all our neighbors live and we are neighborly."

"Oh," said Pooh, not quite understanding. "It *is* a splendid day in it, isn't it?"

"Quite," said Owl. "Now I am off for an owl's-eye view!" He flew up and circled once around Pooh's house.

"What does the neighbor—er—what does it look like from up there?" called Pooh.

"I can see the Hundred-Acre Wood spread out below me," shouted Owl. "I say, I think I see your closest neighbor, Piglet, out raking leaves!"

"Hmm," thought Pooh.
"That reminds me that I wanted
to visit Piglet today."
    And so, as Owl flew off, Pooh decided he would bring
a neighborly present to his closest neighbor, Piglet.

Pooh tucked a honeypot under his arm and walked down the path toward Piglet's house. But halfway there he had a thought: "I *could* take this path straight to Piglet's house. Or—I could take the long way about and try to find this thing Owl called our neighborhood. And sooner or later the path would take me to Piglet's house, anyway."

And that is what he did.

After a while, Pooh came to the house where Kanga and Roo lived.

"Hello, Kanga," said Pooh. "I'm bringing a present to Piglet, but I'm going the long way to try to find our neighborhood."

"Oh, of course," said Kanga kindly. "Perhaps you'd like to join us for a snack along the way."

Pooh *was* feeling a bit eleven o'clockish, so they all went past the sandy pit where Roo liked to play and up to the picnic spot.

One picnic basket and a lot of honey later, Pooh thanked Kanga and Roo and headed down the path toward Rabbit's house.

"Hello, Rabbit!" called Pooh. "I'm taking the long way to Piglet's house to give him this neighborly present. By the way, have you seen any other neighbors about?"

"I am your neighbor!" said Rabbit.

"Oh, yes, of course," said Pooh.

"Since you're here," Rabbit continued, "would you mind taking these carrots to Christopher Robin? I promised he'd have them in time for lunch."

"I'd be happy to," Pooh said.

Pooh marched along with carrots under one arm and a honeypot under the other. After crossing slopes of heather and steep banks of sandstone, Pooh arrived, tired and hungry, at Christopher Robin's door.

"Thank you for delivering my carrots," said Christopher Robin. "Why don't you join me for lunch?"

"I am on
my way to bring
Piglet a neighborly
present," answered Pooh.
"But I don't see why I couldn't stop, just for a little while."
    After a lunch of more honey and a longish snooze,
Pooh went back to looking for the neighborhood as he
headed to Piglet's house.

He walked down the path and through a little pine wood and climbed over the gate to Eeyore's house.

"Hello, Eeyore," said Pooh. "I was just on my way to have a neighborly visit with Piglet."

"Not coming to visit me," said Eeyore. "I didn't think so. Why, only four days ago Tigger bounced me on his way to the swimming hole. How many neighborly visits can you expect, really?"

"Oh, are you my neighbor, too?" asked Pooh.

"I suppose," Eeyore replied.

Pooh, feeling rather bad now, offered Eeyore a nice lick of honey.

Pooh opened the jar. Eeyore peered in and sighed.

Pooh took a look. "Oh, bother! Empty," he said.

"I don't mind," said Eeyore. "But what about Piglet?"

Pooh walked off glumly, trying to think how he was going to tell Piglet about the neighborly present Piglet was not going to get.

Just then Pooh saw Owl flying by.

"I believe I may have seen our neighborhood, although I'm not too sure," Pooh told him. "But now I have no neighborly present left for Piglet."

"Well, I say now! You, sir, are in a bit of a tight spot, aren't you? Perhaps you can get a fill-up at the old bee tree," suggested Owl.

"That's a good idea, Owl, but it's such a long way,"
sighed Pooh.

"Yes, yes, yes," said Owl. "I suggest you follow
someone such as myself to find the wisest and quickest
way through the neighborhood."

So Pooh, being a bear of very little brain, decided to follow Owl (who was an owl of substantially more brain) to the old bee tree. Pooh could hear a loud buzzing near the top of the tree.

Up, up, up
Pooh climbed.

"Splendid! Keep it up, Pooh Bear!" called Owl. "Past
the bees. To the very top of the tree. Now, look all
around you. What do you see?"

The Hundred-Acre Wood was spread out below Pooh.

"Oh, look! I can see everyone!" cried Pooh excitedly. "The whole Hundred-Acre Wood!"

"Exactly!" shouted Owl, who couldn't hear very well from so far below. "It's the whole neighborhood!"

"So that's what our neighborhood is!" thought Pooh. "It's been right in front of me all along."

Sandy Pit Where
Roo Plays

Pooh's House

Piglet's
House

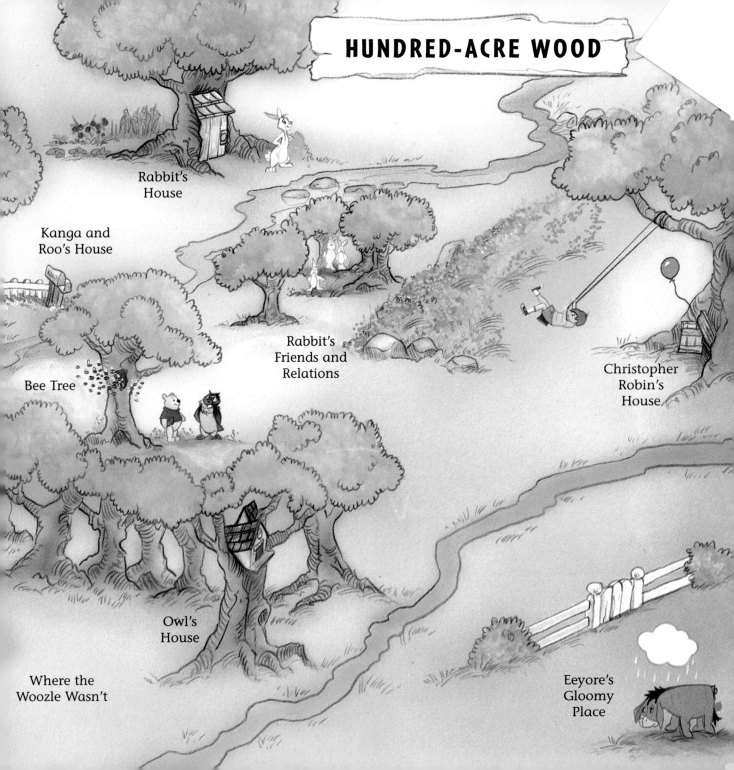

HUNDRED-ACRE WOOD

Rabbit's
House

Kanga and
Roo's House

Rabbit's
Friends and
Relations

Bee Tree

Christopher
Robin's
House

Owl's
House

Where the
Woozle Wasn't

Eeyore's
Gloomy
Place

And after Pooh had refilled his honeypot, he and Owl did the very neighborly thing of going to Piglet's house for supper.